The Twins & Tabiffa

This 1993 edition is published by Gramercy Books,
distributed by Outlet Book Company, Inc.
a Random House Company,
40 Engelhard Avenue
Avenel, New Jersey 07001

Random House
New York • Toronto • London • Sydney • Auckland

Designed by Kathryn Wolgast

Printed and bound in Singapore

Library of Congress Cataloging-in-Publication Data

Heward, Constance.
The twins and Tabiffa / by Constance Heward ; illustrated by
Susan Beatrice Pearse.
p. cm.
Originally published: Philadelphia : George W. Jacobs, 1923.
Summary: Twins Binkie and Dinkie and their big brother Peter value their
black cat Tabiffa more than any other family members do, but Tabiffa proves her
worth when the house catches fire.
ISBN 0-517-09352-9
[1. Cats—Fiction. 2. Twins—Fiction. 3. Brothers—Fiction.
4. Fires—Fiction.] I. Pearse, Susan Beatrice, ill. II. Title.
PZ7.H445Tv 1993
[E]—dc20 93-15524
CIP
AC

8 7 6 5 4 3 2 1

The Twins & Tabiffa

Told in Words by
Constance Heward

Told in Pictures by
Susan Beatrice Pearse

Derrydale • New York • Avenel, New Jersey

Tabiffa was a big black cat with a coat like velvet, a beautiful tail, and handsome whiskers. She walked daintily, like a princess.

She belonged partly to Peter, who was seven years old — a thin boy with red hair and freckles.

But mostly she belonged to Binkie and Dinkie. They were twins, four years old, with round faces and black hair which looked in front as if it had been nibbled by a mouse. They were exactly alike, so, to tell one from the other, Binkie always wore red and Dinkie always wore blue.

Now, one day a dreadful thing happened. Tabiffa disappeared and Binkie and Dinkie cried and cried and cried, until their cheeks got all big and puffy and nearly buried their eyes.

Mother hugged them and kissed them and said she would go to the pet store and buy a new cat, but Binkie and Dinkie said they wanted Tabiffa.

Nurse said it was a good riddance, because she didn't care for cats in the nursery.

And Father came in with his slipper, and said if they didn't stop crying at once he would spank them. (But they knew he would never do it.)

They stopped crying then, and Peter took them to search the house for Tabiffa, although he knew she wasn't in it because he had looked in every room and closet more than once that day.

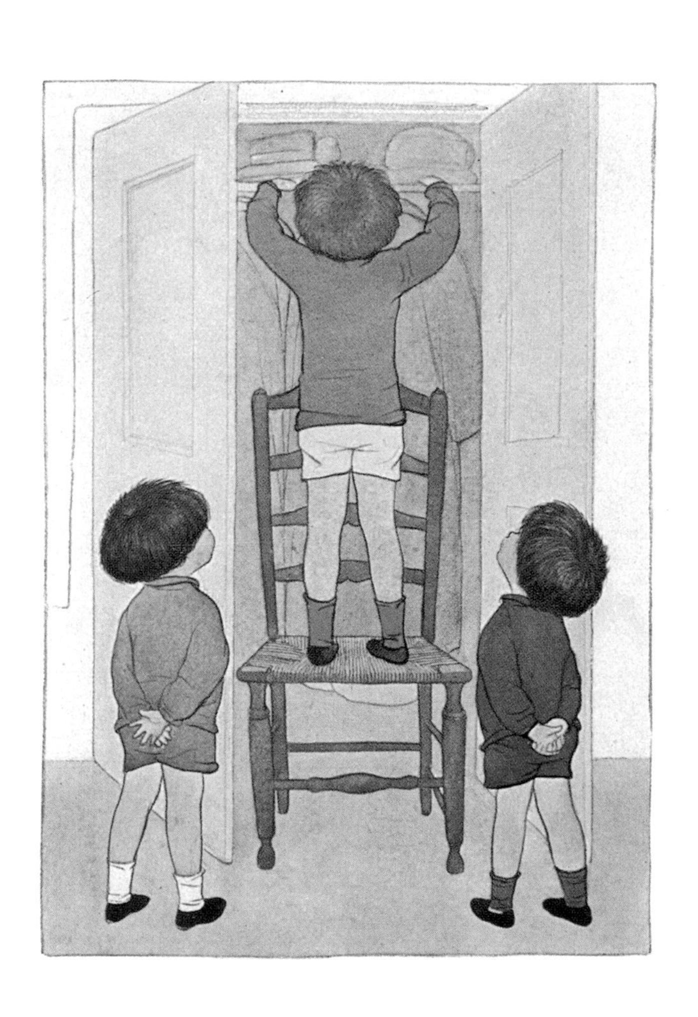

For a whole week Tabiffa was lost and Binkie and Dinkie were so sad that they began to look pale and thin.

But one night, after the twins had cried themselves to sleep, Peter lay in his bed beside theirs and racked his brain for a plan to get Tabiffa back.

And while he lay there something came softly in through the half-open door. It was Tabiffa, and in her mouth she carried a small black kitten.

She sprang onto Binkie and Dinkie's bed. She scraped a nice little nest in the comforter near the foot of the bed and put the kitten gently into it.

Then she went away looking very large and black and important, while Peter sat up in bed hugging himself with excitement because he was sure that she had gone to get more kittens.

And he was right, for she brought them, one at a time, in her mouth, until there were four little, soft, black, mewing things in the nest in the comforter.

Then Tabiffa curled herself up beside them, purring loudly. Peter got out of bed and was just going to wake the twins, when Nurse came walking into the room.

When she saw Tabiffa and her kittens on the bed she was very angry and she scolded Peter for being out of bed. She scolded so hard that Binkie and Dinkie woke up.

"She's come back!" screamed Binkie.

"Wif some dear little babies!" screamed Dinkie, and they knelt at the foot of the bed, and kissed Tabiffa and never even heard Nurse's scolding.

But Father and Mother did, and they came up to see what could be happening.

Binkie and Dinkie rushed at them and hugged them around their knees, and begged and begged that Tabiffa and the kittens might stay, while Peter tried to explain at the top of his voice how Tabiffa had brought them, and Nurse said she never knew such goings-on.

The end of it was that Tabiffa and the kittens were put into an old workbasket, with a piece of blanket in it, on the floor beside the twins' bed. And everybody went to sleep, full of happiness.

Except Nurse, and her face under her nightcap was enough to turn the milk sour, if there had been any near enough.

Now, in the very middle of the night, when the moon was peeping in at the windows, Peter was awakened by something poking and patting his face. He was dreadfully frightened until he heard a loud, pitiful "Miaow! Miaow-ow-ow!" right in his ear, and he knew it was Tabiffa.

As he tried to push her away, his eyes smarted and he smelled smoke. He jumped out of bed and ran to Nurse and shouted in her ear that the house was on fire.

Then he ran to wake Father and Mother, and the children were bundled up in blankets and carried onto the lawn, and Nurse's nightcap had come off and her curling-pins were showing.

And Mrs. Moriarty, the cook, came running out, holding her pet frying pan under her arm.

And Susan, the housemaid, came out in a raincoat and bare feet and her best Sunday hat in a green paper bag.

And they all stood and watched the smoke come curling out of the attic windows, and Tabiffa sat in her basket with the kittens in it and watched it, too.

And then the fire engine dashed wildly up, and the firemen ran up ladders and squirted great streams of water out of their hoses onto the fire, and it did not take very long to put it out.

But the children went to sleep in their blankets on the summer-house floor, with their feet in the middle like soldiers in a tent.

Tabiffa wears a beautful red leather collar now with a silver plate on it, and on the plate is written: "I am Tabiffa, who saved the house from burning."

Her four kittens are getting dreadfully big, but they still sleep in the basket by Binkie and Dinkie's bed, although it is a tightish fit. And Tabiffa makes a little nest for herself at the foot of the bed.